I WONDER WHAT'S UNDER
by Doris Herold Lund   pictures by Janet McCaffery

Parents' Magazine Press

New York

To ERIC and MARK

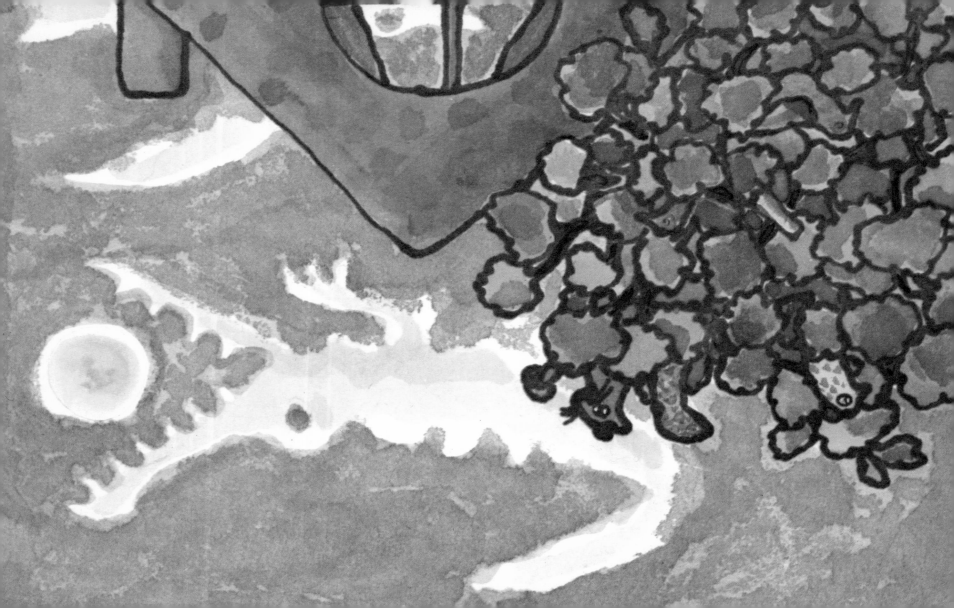

"I wonder what's under
my bed,"
Dudley said.

"It's late,"
said his father.
"Time to go to sleep.
Whatever is under your bed
will keep."

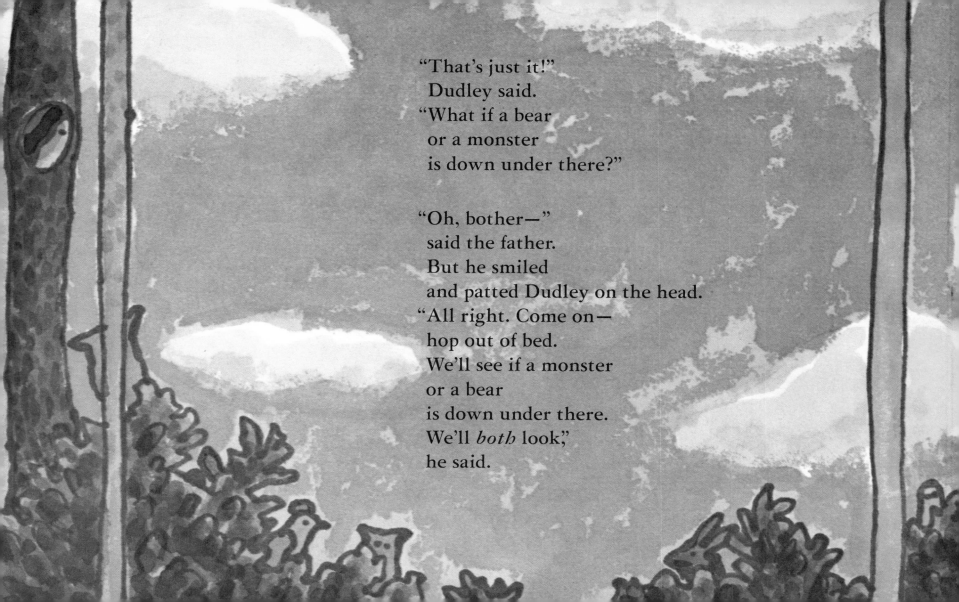

"That's just it!"
Dudley said.
"What if a bear
or a monster
is down under there?"

"Oh, bother—"
said the father.
But he smiled
and patted Dudley on the head.
"All right. Come on—
hop out of bed.
We'll see if a monster
or a bear
is down under there.
We'll *both* look,"
he said.

With that,
Dudley sprang out of bed
and lay down on the floor
flat.

His father got down
on one knee.
"Well, Dudley,"
he said at last,
"what do you see?"

"My coloring book!"
yelled Dudley. "Look!
The coloring book
I lost last week!"

Then he ducked his head,
wiggled back under the bed again
and gave a happy shriek.
"And my water gun—
my favorite one!
Boy, oh boy,
now I can have some fun!"

"Dudley," said his father,
"that's fine.
Tomorrow you can have some fun.
Now it's almost nine..."

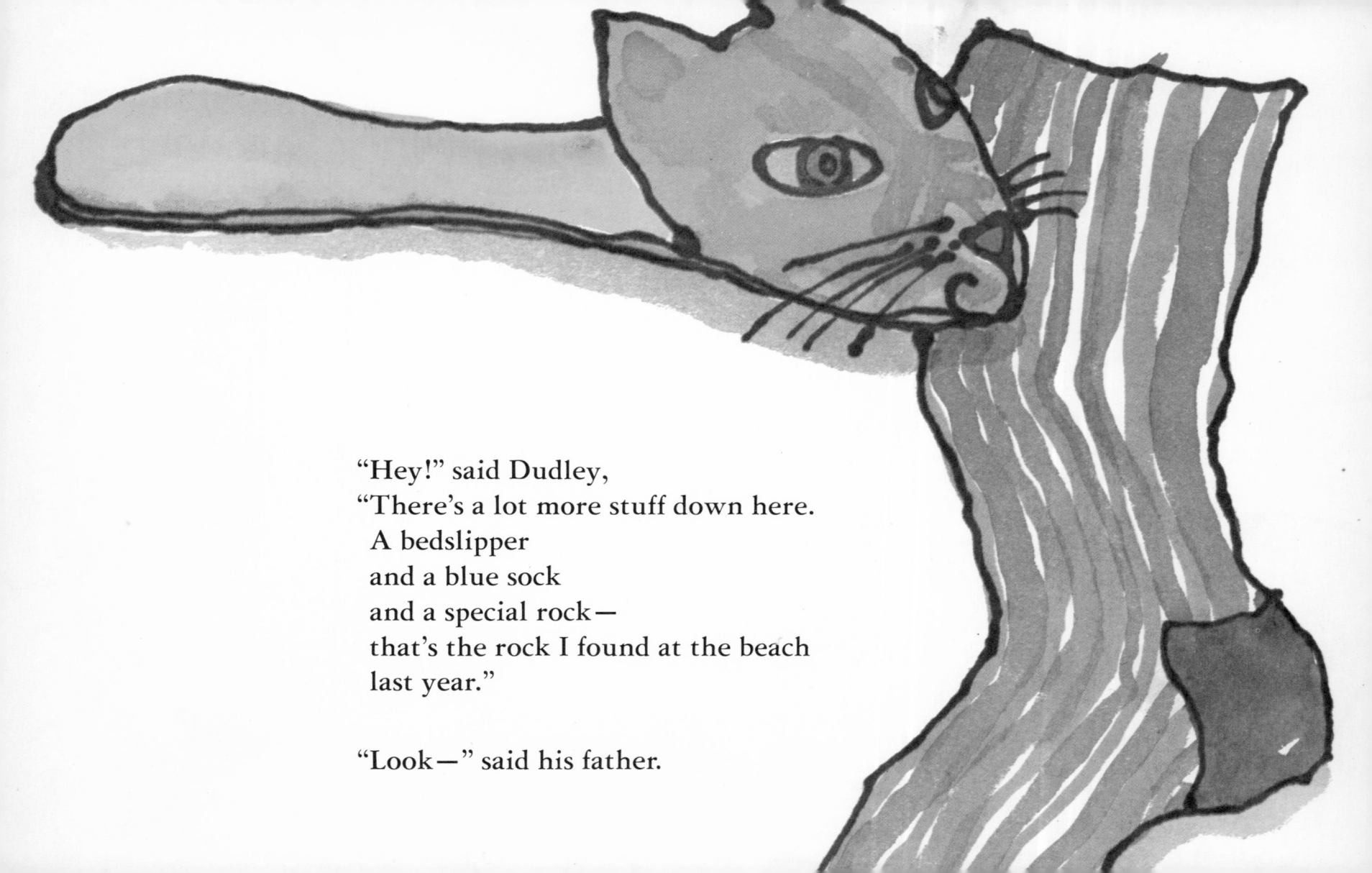

"Hey!" said Dudley,
"There's a lot more stuff down here.
 A bedslipper
 and a blue sock
 and a special rock—
 that's the rock I found at the beach
 last year."

"Look—" said his father.

"I *am* looking—"
said Dudley under the bed.
"I just found three marbles.
A green one. A blue one.
And a red.

"And here's my pencil.
And here's my new pen!"

"Dudley," said his father,
"In the morning
you can look under the bed again.
Now—"

"Wow!"
cried Dudley.
"I just found a dime!"
He crawled out, smiling.
"Now I'll go to bed."

"It's about time,"
   Dudley's father said.

"Goodnight,"
   said the father,
   and he bent down to give him a hug.
   Then he walked toward the door…

"Daddy?" said the little boy,
"just one thing more—
   I wonder what's under the *rug*
   that's under my bed."

"Oh, no!"
   Dudley's tired father said.

Dudley sat up.
"I know there's not a bear
or a monster—
there's not even room
for a puppy down there.
What I'm worried about the most…"

"Yes?" said his father.

"Suppose there's a ghost?
I mean, ghosts are sort of flat.
They could slide under the rug
and just wait—
like that."

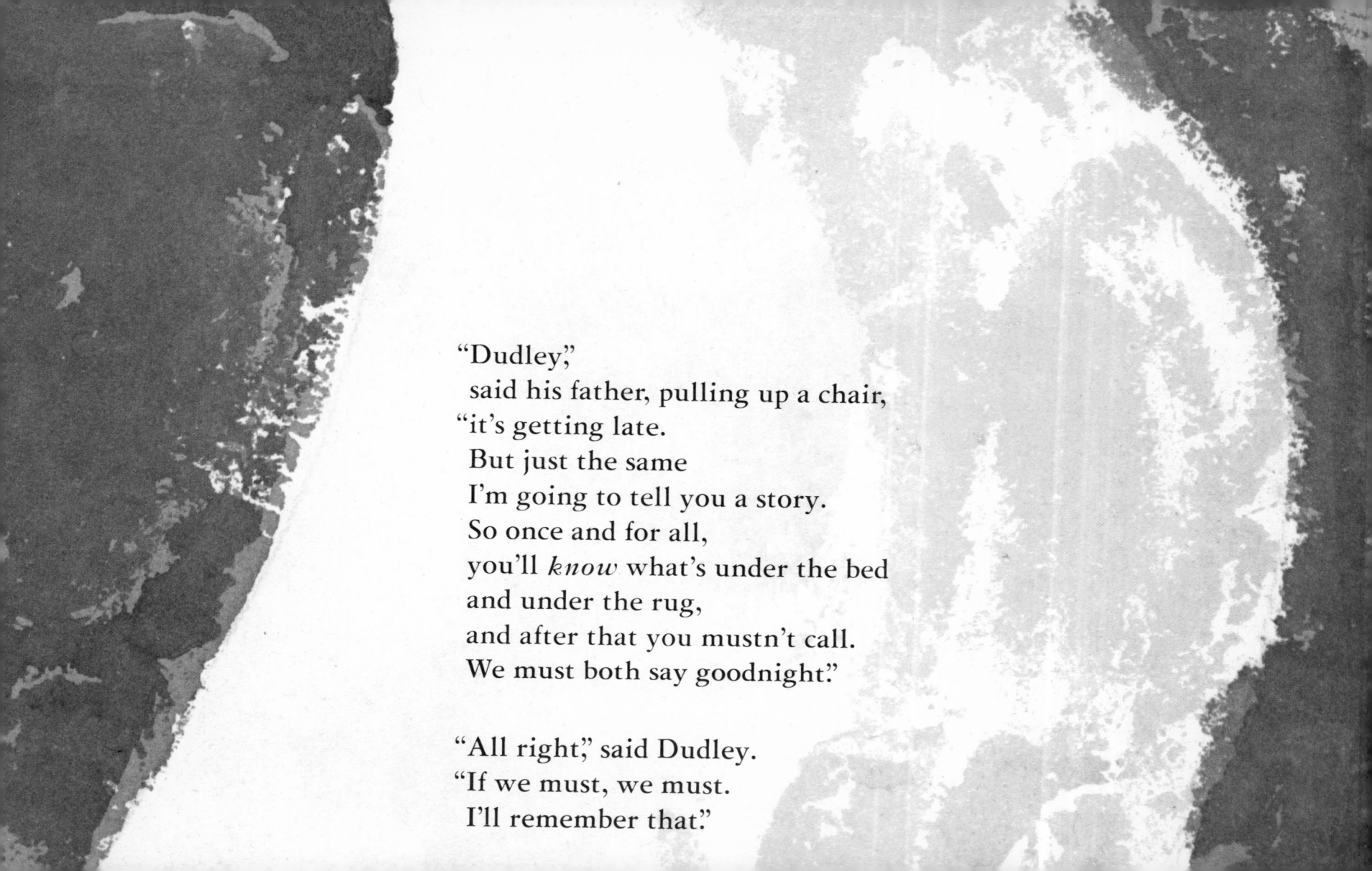

"Dudley,"
 said his father, pulling up a chair,
"it's getting late.
 But just the same
 I'm going to tell you a story.
 So once and for all,
 you'll *know* what's under the bed
 and under the rug,
 and after that you mustn't call.
 We must both say goodnight."

"All right," said Dudley.
"If we must, we must.
 I'll remember that."

"First of all,"
said the father,
"under the rug there's dust..."

"Why?" said Dudley.

"I don't know," sighed his father.
"But under the rug
  there's usually dust.
  And under the dust
  there's the floor.
  And that's what the floor is for—
  to hold up the dust
  and your rug and your bed…"

"And me?" Dudley asked.

"And you!"
  smiled his father.
"The floor holds me up, too.
  But under the floor is a ceiling—
  the ceiling of another room."

"*What* room?" asked Dudley.

"Well, where do we have a sink
  and a stove
  and a frying pan
  and a broom? Can you think?"
"The kitchen!" Dudley cried.

"The kitchen. Yes.
    Where bacon and eggs are fried,"
    Dudley's father said.
"And under the kitchen ceiling
    is a light
    that hangs right over your head
    when you're at the table—"

"Where I eat eggs!
  And jelly and bread!"
  shouted Dudley.

"You're right," Dudley's father said.
"Because under the table
  is a chair—
  and you sit right there."

"I like this story,"
  said Dudley.
"It's neat.
  There's lots and lots about me.
  But what's under my feet?"

"The floor,
once more.
Only this time it's a tile floor—
of squares.
Some are white. Some are brown."

"Never mind what color,"
said Dudley. "Who cares?
Let's keep going down.
I want to know what's under those squares
on the kitchen floor.
Any bears?"

"No bears," said his father.
"Another ceiling.
Under the squares
is the cellar ceiling...

"and I've a feeling
if you looked around, you might
find a spider
spinning her web
under the shelf where we store potatoes
and apple cider.

"...or maybe a mouse somewhere,"
Dudley's father went on.
"But you won't find a bear
or a monster anywhere
in this house.
It's only a mouse who really likes
to live in a house."

"I'm not afraid of a mouse,"
Dudley said.
His father nodded his head.
"Good."

"But," Dudley said with a great big yawn,
"please go on.
Now tell me what's under that shelf..."

"Our pile of wood.
Remember when we chopped down the birch
and the big old willow?"

Dudley's head sank deeper in his pillow.
"But then...what's under...
our woodpile?"
he asked. His eyes were closing.
His mouth wore a sleepy smile.

"The cellar floor."
Dudley's father got up softly.
Once more
he walked over to the door.

"It's concrete," he said.
"It feels cold and scratchy
on bare feet."

"And under the cellar floor?
Under my feet?"
whispered Dudley.

"There's dirt...

"there's the earth...

"there's the *world!*
So now you know,"
Dudley's father said.

With that, Dudley curled
up in a warm little ball
and tucked his arms under his head.
And he didn't call
his father back from the door
any more at all...

For he didn't have to wonder
what was under his bed.
He *knew.*

THE END

DORIS HEROLD LUND is a free-lance copywriter, commercial artist and the mother of four children. She is also the author of three other popular books on the Parents' Magazine Press list: *Attic of the Wind, Did You Ever?* and *Did You Ever Dream?* Mrs. Lund was born in Indiana and is a graduate of Swarthmore College. She now makes her home in Vero Beach, Florida.

JANET McCAFFERY and her husband live in New York City but enjoy spending their summers in northern New Jersey. Here Mrs. McCaffery gardens and rides her bicycle through the countryside—always carrying a sketch pad with her. Among the many delightful books she has illustrated for children are *The Swamp Witch, The Traveling Ball of String,* and *Mermaid of Stones.*